art direction **susie garland rice**
layout **shannon osborne thompson**

All art and editorial material is owned by Dalmatian Press.

ISBN: 1-57759-221-2

First published in the United States in 1999 by Dalmatian Press, U.S.A.

The 3 Little Pigs

retold by
john duncan

illustrated by
wes ware

Dalmatian Press

Once there were three little pigs.
They set out into the great, big forest to look
for a nice spot to build homes for themselves.

The third little pig gathered up
bricks to build his house,
"ploppety, cloppety, clop."

The first two pigs finished their houses in no time. They said to the third pig, "You're working too hard, why don't you come play?" But he kept right on building, "Clink, clonk, plop, swack."

Finally, he was all finished. He relaxed by a warm fire in his safe and strong house.

One day a big, bad wolf came to the straw house of the first little pig. He could smell a kettle of soup and it made him very hungry. He said, "Little pig, little pig, let me in." But the first little pig replied, "Not by the hair of my chinny chin chin."

So the wolf said, "Then I'll huff and I'll puff and I'll blow your house down." With a "swoosh and a woosh" the straw house blew away. The first little pig jumped up and ran all the way to the second pig's house.

The next day the big, bad wolf came to the house of the second little pig. He could smell a fresh loaf of bread baking in the oven. "He said little pig, little pig, let me in." But the second little pig replied, "Not by the hair of our chinny chin chins."

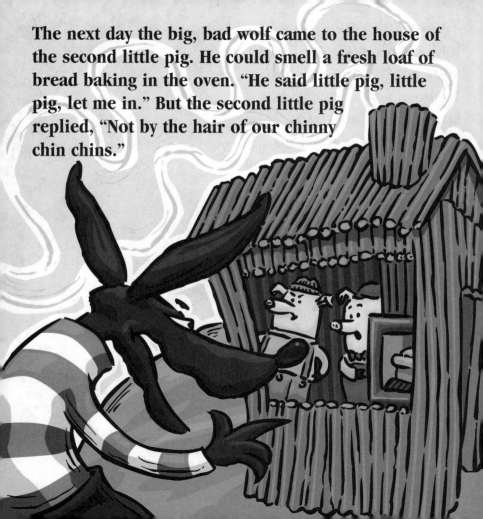

So the wolf said, "Then I'll huff and I'll puff and I'll blow your house down." With a gust of air and a "crack and crash" the stick house fell to the ground. Both pigs jumped up and ran all the way to the third little pig's house.

When the third little pig heard about the wolf he was glad his brothers were safe and he said, "You must be hungry and tired, sit down and have some pie."

So the wolf said, "Then I'll huff and I'll puff and I'll blow your house down." He puffed and puffed and blew with all his might but the brick house wouldn't fall down. So he gruffed and snuffed and blew and blew again but the brick house just wouldn't fall.

The wolf had never had this happen before.
He sat down on an old log and began to cry.

The third little pig said, "There, there Mr. Wolf, you don't have to be so sad. You have a remarkable talent and there are much better things to do than just blowing down houses."

Outside the woods they heard
the sounds of children laughing
and playing. It was the local fair
and everyone was going.

The three little pigs and the big, sad wolf all went down to the fair. "Here's a wonderful way to use your gift," said the third little pig.

With a huff and a puff the wolf started blowing up colorful balloons for all the children, "Sssssssssss!"

They came from miles around to see all the sizes and shapes. The wolf was so happy and amazed at all his new friends. He wasn't bad or sad anymore. He was the big, glad wolf.

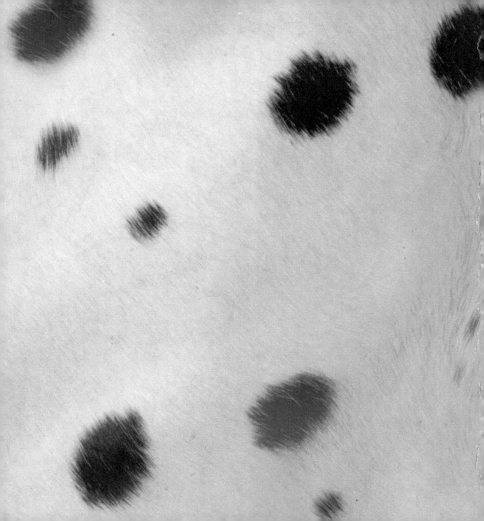